Dear Molly, Dear Olive

Olive Finds Treasure
(of the Most Precious Kind)

written by
Megan Atwood

illustrated by
Lucy Fleming

PICTURE WINDOW BOOKS
a capstone imprint

Dear Molly, Dear Olive is published by Picture Window Books,
a Capstone Imprint
1710 Roe Crest Drive
North Mankato, Minnesota 56003
www.mycapstone.com

Library of Congress Cataloging-in-Publication Data
Names: Atwood, Megan, author. | Fleming, Lucy, illustrator.
Title: Olive finds treasure (of the most precious kind) / by Megan Atwood;
[illustrated by Lucy Fleming].
Description: North Mankato, Minnesota: Picture Window Books, an
imprint of Capstone Press, [2017] | Series: Dear Molly, Dear Olive |
Summary: Pen pals Molly and Olive consider themselves best friends
even though they have never actually met because Molly lives in New
York City and Olive lives on a farm in Iowa—but when Olive finds a
diamond bracelet in the grass the two girls start to wonder if they can
finally get the money for one of them to visit the other.
Identifiers: LCCN 2016010939 | ISBN 9781479586936 (library binding) |
ISBN 9781623706159 (paperback) | ISBN 9781479586974 (ebook (pdf))
Subjects: LCSH: Best friends—Juvenile fiction. | Pen pals—Juvenile
fiction. | Letter writing—Juvenile fiction. | Lost articles—Juvenile
fiction. | Conduct of life—Juvenile fiction. | New York (N.Y.)—
Juvenile fiction. | Iowa—Juvenile fiction. | CYAC: Best friends—
Fiction. | Friendship—Fiction. | Pen pals—Fiction. | Letter writing—
Fiction. | Lost and found possessions—Fiction. | Conduct of life—
Fiction. | New York (N.Y.)—Fiction. | Iowa—Fiction. .
Classification: LCC PZ7.A8952 Ol 2017 | DDC 813.6—dc23
LC record available at http://lccn.loc.gov/2016010939

Designers: Aruna Rangarajan and Tracy McCabe

Design Elements: Shutterstock

Printed in Canada.
009642F16

Table of Contents

Dear Molly,
Dear Olive

Molly and Olive are best friends — best friends who've never met! Two years ago, in second grade, they signed up for a cross-country Pen Pal Club. Their friendship was instant.

Molly and Olive send each other letters and email. They send postcards, notes, and little gifts too. Molly lives in New York City with her mom and younger brother. Olive lives on a farm near Sergeant Bluff, Iowa, with her parents. The girls' lives are very different from one another. But Molly and Olive understand each other better than anyone.

Chapter 1

Lots of Sparkle

Olive

Racie kicked the ball to me, and I missed it. Like usual. Ugh! Soccer and I weren't good friends at all.

I wished I could just stick with gymnastics. But my mom and dad said I needed to "branch out" when the season was over. Try something new. So I was trying soccer. Boy, it sure wasn't going well.

Coach clapped and yelled, "It's okay, Olive! Get it next time!"

I ran to get the ball for the 800th time. Once I stood across from Racie again, Coach tried to help. "Now pass it back to her, Olive," she said. "Use the inside of your foot, like this."

She showed me, and I drew back my foot and . . . whiffed the ball.

My face burned. I saw Racie try to hide a smile. But I tried again, and I did it! It barely got to Racie, but it got there. Coach gave me a thumbs-up. Then she went to the next pair of kids.

"You're doing good for your first time!" Racie said.

I nodded, but I wished that practice would FINALLY be over. My best friend, Molly, played soccer too, in New York. I hadn't told her yet that I'd started playing. Soccer would give us one more thing to talk about — even though we never ran out of stuff to talk about. I touched my necklace — the one she'd given me — and smiled.

Coach blew the whistle. We were done. Racie jogged over to me. She put out her hand for a low five. "Hey, seriously," she said, "you did great."

AWESOME

"Thanks, Racie," I said. "I'm sorry my passes were so bad."

She shrugged and patted my shoulder.

Ugh.

I saw Dad's truck in the parking lot. He'd told me we had to leave quick after practice. We were going to milk the goats together. Then he had to fix a fence.

I grabbed my bag and ran across the field. My bag looked like a giant purple sausage.

It wouldn't even zip all the way. My grandma's hand-knitted sweater was stuffed inside it. I had gotten too hot during the day, so I'd shoved the sweater in my bag after putting on my soccer clothes.

"See you Wednesday, Olive!" Racie yelled.

I groaned. Another practice. Saturdays and Wednesdays were practice days. Fridays were game days. It was going to be a long season.

Just before I reached the parking lot, something twinkled in the grass. I put down my bag and stopped to look. Even though my dad was waiting, I had to check it out.

 It was a bracelet. With diamonds!

The sun sparkled off every gem. There were at least twelve of them. I looked around to see if anyone saw me. No one was paying attention. Dad was looking down at his phone.

The bracelet was the most beautiful thing I'd ever seen. I swallowed. I knew I should tell Coach about it. Or my dad. But something made me stop. Instead I tucked the bracelet into my sock, to the side of my shin guard.

A long honk made me jump. I grabbed my bag again and sprinted to the truck.

"Come on, Peanut," Dad said. "Let's go! How was practice? Are you glad you went after all?"

Thinking of the bracelet in my sock, I said, "I really am, Dad."

Chapter 2

Birthday Plans

Molly

I reread the email from Olive.

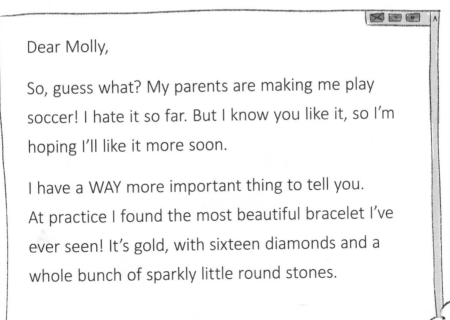

Dear Molly,

So, guess what? My parents are making me play soccer! I hate it so far. But I know you like it, so I'm hoping I'll like it more soon.

I have a WAY more important thing to tell you. At practice I found the most beautiful bracelet I've ever seen! It's gold, with sixteen diamonds and a whole bunch of sparkly little round stones.

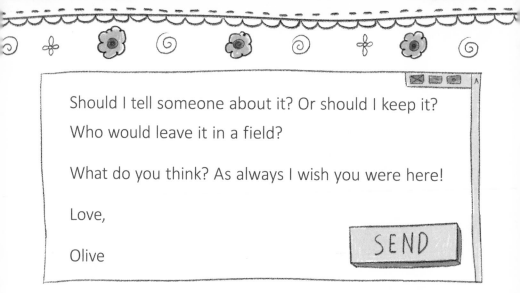

Should I tell someone about it? Or should I keep it? Who would leave it in a field?

What do you think? As always I wish you were here!

Love,

Olive

SEND

I chewed on my lip and bounced my leg. A bracelet. Full of diamonds. That had to cost a million dollars.

"Molly! Damien!" Mom yelled from the kitchen. She could yell louder than anyone I knew. My little brother and I were late again for dinner. She'd already called us twice.

I shut my laptop and ran out of my room. I needed time to think about Olive's treasure before I wrote her back. My little brother rushed past me in the hallway.

"Watch out!" I yelled.

Damien stuck out his tongue at me and slid into the kitchen.

I smelled dinner and wrinkled my nose. Fish and broccoli. The grossest dinner in the world.

"I see your face, Ms. Molly, and that'll be enough of that," Mom said.

EWW!

YUCK

"We have to eat healthy now," she continued. "If we do, then we can eat tons of cake for your birthday. Right, Molly?"

I smiled. She was right. My birthday! I dug into the fish. "One more week!" I said. That seemed like forever away.

"Let's go over the plan to make sure we have it right, okay?" Mom said. "So we're having your party at the community center park. And we're renting a moon bounce."

That thought made me bounce up and down in my seat. I couldn't WAIT for that.

"People can also play soccer if they want," Mom said. "The field is right there."

This thought stopped my bouncing. I wished SO HARD that Olive could come. I could show her what I liked about soccer. She didn't seem to like it too much right now.

"We'll get you a gigantic chocolate and white cake —"

"No flowers on it!" I said.

"No flowers on it," Mom said. "Maybe a soccer ball?"

I nodded and shoved in more fish. Then some broccoli. It all tasted really good now for some reason.

"Maybe a few more games," Mom

said. "How about four square and pin the tail on the donkey?"

"I don't know about the donkey one," I said. "But we need a candy table."

Mom winked at me. "Got it."

I looked down at my plate. All my food was gone. I thought about my classmates coming to my birthday party. I thought about how I would beat the boys at soccer and then everyone at four square. I thought about how much candy I would eat. . . .

But then I got sad. My tenth birthday. The birthday when I hit double digits. It was a huge deal. And my best friend in the world wouldn't be there.

"What's wrong, Molly?" Mom asked.

"I just wish Olive could come to my party, that's all," I said.

Mom got up and picked up her plate. She put one arm around me and squeezed. "I know," she said. "I'm sorry. But it's quite a trip to get here from Iowa."

She picked up my plate and Damien's. "Damien, your turn to load the dishwasher," she said.

My brother groaned and slid off his chair. He walked by me and stepped on my foot, on purpose. But I didn't care. Something my mom had said got me thinking. Maybe there WAS a way to get Olive to my birthday party.

I ran to my room to send an email.

Chapter 3

Olive Loses It

Olive

Molly always had great ideas. This time was no different.

Hi, Olive!

I have the most perfect idea ever.

Whoever had that bracelet wasn't a very good bracelet owner, right? I mean, what was it doing on a soccer field? I think you were SUPPOSED to find it! Maybe the person doesn't want the bracelet anymore.

So here's the plan: Why don't you SELL the bracelet and buy a plane ticket to New York for my birthday party? It's perfect! That bracelet must be worth a lot. What do you think?

Love,

Molly

I wanted to go to Molly's birthday party SO BAD. I couldn't think of anything better.

See, Molly and I are best friends, but we've never met in person. I've seen tons of pictures of her, of course. And she has seen a ton of me. But it's just not the same as being there.

Molly was right. Whoever left that bracelet didn't take good care of it. My mom and dad always taught me to keep track of my things, and I did. I wrote Molly back.

Dear Molly,

I think that is a PERFECT idea. I want to go to your birthday party! Ten is really special. I'm dying to see you in person too! If I sell the bracelet and buy the plane ticket, our parents will have to say yes, right?

I stopped for a second. My parents would NOT like me buying a plane ticket on my own. But once I had it, what could they do?

How should I sell it? And how do I buy a plane ticket? One thing at a time, I guess, like my dad says.

I love this idea! Thank you so much. If all goes well, I'll see you in a week!

XOXOXOXO,

Olive

I got up and did a little happy dance. This had to work. This just had to work! Suddenly I felt someone near me. I looked over. It was Dad. He was doing a happy dance with me. I was in such a good mood I kept dancing, and Dad did too.

"I love a happy dance!" he said. "I don't know why we're doing it, but I love it!"

My mom peeked around the corner of my room. "Hey!" she said. "A dance party!" Pretty soon all of us were giggling and breathing hard.

After a few minutes, Mom said, "Olive, I came in to

grab that pretty sweater Grandma made you.
I wanted to fix the hole for you."

"Thanks, Mom," I said. "That hole's been
there forever."

"I know. You wear it so much you're going
to wear it out."

"I love that sweater," I said. "It makes me
not miss Grandma quite so much."

I lifted the duffel bag onto
my bed. But something
was wrong. I stuck my
hands in. Grandma's
sweater wasn't there.

I'd lost it.

SEND MORE MAIL

Bobby's Beautiful Baubles

☆ GOOD LUCK ☆

Chapter 4

One Thing at a Time

Molly

"She might come!" I said out loud to no one. "What am I saying? She IS coming!"

OLIVE WAS COMING TO MY BIRTHDAY PARTY! My dreams were coming true.

Except a couple small things first. We had to sell the bracelet and get a plane ticket. One thing at a time, like Olive said.

I tried to think hard about where we could sell the bracelet. People sold and bought things on the Internet all the time. But my mom had warned me about that kind of thing. It'd be safer to sell it in person. It had to be a business. A real store that Olive could visit.

After a few online searches, I found a place near Sergeant Bluff, Iowa. It was called Bobby's Beautiful Baubles. But how much money would we need to get for the bracelet?

I did a search for "plane ticket, Sergeant Bluff, Iowa, New York City." There were no tickets out of Sergeant Bluff. The town was too small. But there was a flight from Sioux City. Olive had gymnastics there, so it wouldn't be hard for her to get to that city.

The plane ticket cost $525.

Yikes. That was a lot of money. I'd never seen that much in my life! I hoped Bobby's Beautiful Baubles could help us out.

I wrote to Olive and gave her the address. I told her how much money she needed to get. Now all she had to do was go to Bobby's, be brave, and sell that bracelet!

Chapter 5

Bobby's Beautiful Baubles

Olive

I'd printed Molly's email and brought it along. I reread it now and took a deep breath. I was standing outside Bobby's Beautiful Baubles, and I did not feel brave at all.

I'd talked my mom into taking me to Sioux City with her after school. She went into town every once in a while to get feed for our animals. I hadn't asked to come along since I was little. Shopping for feed was really boring.

But I told her I would look around the rest of the strip mall while she got the feed.

That's where Bobby's Beautiful Baubles was.

I walked in and cleared my throat. I put on my best adult voice. "Excuse me, Bobby," I said to the man behind the desk. "My name's Olive, and I'd like to sell my bracelet."

The man had a huge grin on his face. "You know, Bobby's not here just now, but I can help you," he said. "I'm Seth."

I reached into my purse and pulled out the

bracelet. The diamonds caught the light in the store. They twinkled. I almost hated to sell it. I also started thinking that this wasn't a good idea. The bracelet wasn't really mine to sell.

But I pushed that thought down and said, "How much for this?"

Seth's eyes got wide. He turned the bracelet in his hands. He whistled. "Where did you get this?" he asked.

"It's mine," I said. I suddenly felt really hot. Sweat started to run down my back.

"Well," he said, "it's awfully pretty. But you have to be eighteen years old to sell things here. Are you eighteen?"

I nodded. "I'm short for my age," I said.

Seth raised an eyebrow. "I see. Then I'll just need to peek at your driver's license. Or a picture ID," he said.

Whoops. I didn't think about that. I didn't have any picture IDs. I was a kid!

I needed to get out of there. Fast. I scooped up the bracelet and put it in my purse again. "Uh, I just . . . I left my ID in the car," I said. "I'll be right back."

Seth nodded. "I'll wait," he said with a smile.

My face burned. I ran out the door.

I felt SO, so dumb. What was I thinking? No grown-up would believe that fancy bracelet was mine. Now what? Time to write Molly with the bad news.

OOPS!

Chapter 6

Molly's Secret Store

So I had to come up with another plan. Olive had written me.

Dear Molly,

The plan failed. They wouldn't buy it. ☹ What should we do now?

XOXO,

Olive

She'd sent me a picture too. Whoa, the bracelet was SO pretty! Whoever lost it must be feeling really bad. But I didn't want to think about that. We needed to sell it. Fast! My party was only days away.

This next part of the new plan . . . well, I wasn't too proud of it.

I took my mom's phone while she was getting ready for work.

I walked to school that morning with the phone in my pocket. At recess I whispered into Lacey's ear, "Tell everyone that I have a super-secret store. And that I have something really big to sell."

I told Lacey because I knew she would gab the quickest.

I marched behind the big slide and waited.

Sure enough, about ten kids came over. I rubbed my hands together. Easy peasy.

"So what exactly is a super-secret store?" Lacey asked.

I leaned in. Everyone else leaned in too. "You all are the lucky few who get to be a part of my Super-Secret Store Recess Time," I said. "During some recesses I'll be selling something really awesome. Do you want to see what's in the store today?"

Everyone nodded. I had their full attention. Cool! I looked around to make sure no one outside our circle was sneaking a peek. Then I took out my mom's phone. I pulled up the picture of the bracelet. The whole crowd made an *ooohhh!* sound.

Yep. My store was already a hit.

After a few seconds, Lacey said, "How do we know that's real?"

"Oh, it's real," I said. "Just look at the way it sparkles. See? Only real diamonds sparkle like that!"

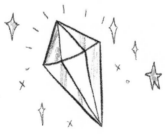

Lacey huffed. "No, not if the DIAMONDS are real. Duh! That the whole THING is real! How do we know you didn't get this picture off the Internet?"

That was a pretty good question. And I didn't have an answer. So I decided to take a chance. "Well, if you don't think it's real, that's fine. I'll just invite other kids to my store." I put the phone in my pocket and yelled, "Show's over! Nothing more to see here!"

The rest of the group grumbled and gave Lacey dirty looks.

"Don't ruin it for the rest of us, Lacey," I heard a boy say.

"I think it's real," a girl said.

"I *know* it's real. Did you see how it sparkled?" another girl said.

Pretty soon the whole crowd was begging to see the bracelet again.

"Who wants to buy it?" I asked, standing tall. Even sour-faced Lacey leaned in again.

"How much is it?" Jenna asked.

"$600," I said.

Everyone stepped back like I'd burped in their faces.

Lacey snorted. "$600! Are you crazy? Where would we get that much money?"

"Well," I said, "I suppose I could take a little less for it." I showed the picture again. "See how pretty it is?"

James, a boy in my class, said, "I have $45 from my birthday. Would you take that?"

A girl said, "I have $120, but it's in the bank. I'd have to ask my mom and dad."

No one had enough money to pay for Olive's plane ticket.

I was getting mad. "You guys, this is a real diamond —" I was cut off as the crowd parted, and Ms. Harter walked up to me. She took one look at the phone in my hand and pointed at the main door.

Time to see Principal Martinez again.

Chapter 7

That Poor Guy

Olive

I still hadn't found my grandma's sweater. It was driving me nuts. I loved that sweater! How could I have lost it?

I was searching my room again, when I heard a knock at the front door. I ran downstairs, but my dad got to the door first.

A nervous man stood outside the door. He fidgeted. "Hi, George," he said, "I hate to bother you. I'm Racie's dad, from soccer."

"Yes! We met at the soccer parent meeting. Come in! What can I do for you, Steven?"

I got a little worried. Maybe he was going to tell Dad that I was ruining soccer for Racie. Because I was so bad.

But Racie's dad said, "It's embarrassing, really. See, I bought my wife a tennis bracelet for our wedding anniversary. But now I can't find it. I think the last time I had it was at soccer practice. I'd just come from the store. When I got home, I saw the latch on the box was loose. I've searched that field a dozen times. I'm hoping someone else picked it up. Did you or Olive find a tennis bracelet?"

My dad shook his head. "I'm so sorry, but we haven't seen anything. Do you want us to go to the field and look again with you?"

"No, that's okay. I've looked everywhere in that field. But if you hear of someone finding a tennis bracelet . . ."

Dad nodded. "Of course. We have your phone number on the soccer list. Good luck. I hope it turns up soon."

I swallowed hard. It wasn't the same bracelet, was it? It couldn't be.

Racie's dad had said *tennis* bracelet. That meant a bracelet with tennis things on it, right? He would have said *diamond* bracelet if it were the same one I'd found.

Later, at dinner, Mom and Dad talked about Racie's dad. "That poor guy," my mom said.

I shrugged. "He should have kept a closer watch on it, if it was so special," I said. I played with the spaghetti on my plate.

Both Mom and Dad stopped talking. Mom put down her fork.

"That's not very nice, Olive," Mom said. "Mistakes happen. Accidents happen. Didn't you just lose your grandma's sweater?"

That stung. Even though she was right, it still made me mad. I pushed my plate back. "What's the big deal? So it's a bracelet with tennis balls on it or something. He can probably get another one really easy."

Mom and Dad looked at each other. Then Dad put down *his* fork. "Honey, a tennis bracelet is a very expensive bracelet. It's a diamond bracelet. It's called a tennis bracelet, but it has nothing to do with the sport. Racie's dad lost a lot of money. And now his wife doesn't get her anniversary gift. It's a sad thing."

And that's when I felt the tears in my eyes.

Chapter 8

Molly Tells the Truth

Molly

Dear Molly,

I feel really terrible. I think I met the owner of the bracelet today. He's the dad of a girl I play soccer with — Racie.

He said he lost a TENNIS bracelet, so I didn't think my bracelet was his. But I guess tennis bracelets are diamond bracelets. Rats.

What do we do? I really want to come to your birthday party. But Racie's dad looked so sad.

Your stealing friend,

Olive

I read the email over and over again. I had a lot of time to read. I was grounded for stealing my mom's phone. No one had believed that I'd "accidentally" put it in my pocket.

Now Olive and I had one more thing in common: stealing.

I was feeling terrible too. I never really thought about the person who lost the bracelet. Now that he was REAL, well . . . our plan didn't seem so great anymore. It felt wrong.

But boy, I sure wanted Olive to come to my birthday party.

Tears fell, and I flopped on the bed, face down, crying into my pillow. I didn't even hear Mom come in. But I felt her warm hand rubbing my back.

Finally, after I'd cried a river, I sat back and wiped my nose on my sleeve. Mom handed me a tissue. I felt a little better.

"You want to tell me what this is all about?" she asked.

I thought about it. Since I was already grounded, what did I have to lose?

"Mom," I said, "Olive found a really pretty bracelet. It has tons of diamonds on it. Real ones. We've been trying to sell it so she can get a plane ticket and come to my birthday party." My voice wobbled at the end of the sentence. Tears started up again.

"I tried to sell it at recess," I continued. "I needed your phone so I could show kids a picture of it. But it didn't work. All my classmates are poor."

Mom made a noise that sounded like a laugh. But then that noise turned into a cough.

"Right," she said. "Most kids don't have money for a diamond bracelet."

I nodded. "Olive just wrote to me. She feels bad because she met the man who lost the bracelet. Now I feel bad too! But, Mom, I'm NEVER going to get to meet Olive. I want her here for my birthday! She's my best friend, and I haven't even talked on the phone with her. It's not fair!"

"I know it's hard," Mom said. "But you and Olive agreed to not talk on the phone or to Skype or anything. You promised to just write to each other."

I nodded. It WAS hard. "Should we just break our promise and call each other?"

Mom looked out the window and slowly nodded. It was her nod that actually meant no. I'd seen it before. "You could do that," she said. "Or you *could* wait a little bit. You've been in tough spots before, right? And you've always made it through okay."

I picked at a thread on my blanket. "Yeah," I said, but I didn't feel real sure of myself.

Mom held my shoulders and looked me right in the eye. "Someday, darling girl, someday you and Olive will meet in person. We'll make it happen. Somehow. But for now I think you and Olive need to do the right thing."

Two fat tears slipped down my face.

"We will," I said.

After Mom left my room, I wrote to Olive.

Hi, Olive,

I feel bad too. You should give back the bracelet.

Love,

Molly

When I hit send, I felt like I'd been punched in the gut.

Chapter 9

Olive Tells the Truth Too

Olive

I hit send. Here's what I'd written:

Dear Molly,

Don't be mad, but I think the right thing to do is give back the bracelet. I PROMISE I'll make it up to you. Please don't be mad.

Love,

Olive

I shut down the computer. I knew Molly was going to be disappointed in me. And pretty soon my parents were going to be disappointed in me too.

I heard the tractor and walked out to the barn. I needed to tell Mom and Dad about finding the bracelet.

I took lots of time to pet the goats first. Then our cat, Stella. Finally I scooped her up in my arms and kept walking to the barn.

The closer we got, though, the more antsy Stella got.

All of a sudden, she jumped out of my arms, scratching my face. I was so surprised, I didn't see the old post hole in front of me. I stepped into the hole and felt my ankle bend . . . the wrong way.

Pain shot up my leg. I yelled.

My ankle felt wrong, wrong, wrong. I tried to pull my foot out, but I couldn't. It was stuck. Tears poured down my face. "Mom!" I yelled, over and over. But the tractor noise drowned me out.

After what felt like forever, the tractor noise stopped. Everything got quiet. All I heard were a couple bleats coming from the goats' pen. "MOM!" I yelled at the top of my lungs.

I couldn't stop crying. The pain had spread all the way up my leg. I fell down in gymnastics all the time. But it had never hurt like this before.

Mom came running to me. "Honey, honey, honey," she said. She looked at my foot in the hole. Then she called my dad's name. He came running too.

"Olive, honey, your ankle is twisted," Mom said. "And your foot is caught on some roots. Your dad and I will need to pull to get you out."

More tears ran down my face. I nodded.

Mom and Dad hooked my arms. "On the count of three," Dad said. "One —"

And then I felt the worst pain ever. I yelled so loud a bunch of birds flew off the branches. But my foot was out. Without my shoe. I could see my ankle now. It was already puffy and bright red.

Dad picked me up. "I don't think it's broken," he said. "But we should get it checked out." Then he put me in the truck, and we all drove to the hospital.

When I got home, Mom and Dad put me on the couch. They propped up my leg. It was a sprain, not a break. Mom got me some ice cream. Dad rubbed my shoulders.

All I kept thinking about was the bracelet.

Racie's dad still didn't have his bracelet back. Also, even if I HAD sold it, I couldn't have gone to New York City with a sprained ankle. It seemed like I was learning a bunch of lessons all at once.

I took a deep breath. "Mom. Dad. I have to tell you something."

Chapter 10

A Better Plan

Molly

Olive's email made me smile.

There was a big reason why we were best friends. We usually thought of the same things at the same time.

But she thought I'd be mad at her! Never.

Hi, Olive,

Are you crazy? I could never be mad at you! Mom says we'll find a time to see each other. Giving the bracelet back makes me feel better. We are doing the right thing.

Love,

Molly

I went to the kitchen to grab a snack. Mom was doing some paperwork. When she saw me, she put down her pen. "Molly," she said, "I've been thinking about you and Olive."

I sat down and swung my legs back and forth. "Oh, the bracelet? Well, Olive sent me an email about giving it back RIGHT when I sent mine. I love

how much we think alike. Everything's okay now. Except I still don't get to see her."

"That's what I want to talk to you about," Mom said. "You and Olive have been so good about sticking to your letter writing. But maybe it's time to make a new agreement. Maybe we can make some . . . changes."

I sat up straight. "You mean, like talking on the phone?"

Mom smiled. "Yes. Or maybe we could even plan a visit."

My legs started tapping on their own. A visit?

Mom could see me getting excited. She put out her hand to slow me down.

"Now, before you get too excited, we need to run this by Olive and her parents. Plus, we need to set up some ground rules. Let's write down our ideas and go from there. Should we do that?"

I jumped up and kept jumping. "Yes! Yes! Yes!" I cried.

When Mom and I finished the plan, I wrote an email.

Hi, Olive,

My mom had the BEST idea. I know we said we'd stick to WRITING ONLY. And it's a great plan. Mostly. But my mom and I thought it was time to change it a bit. If you like the new plan, we can print it off, sign it, and mail it to each other. Like a real contract!

(Mom helped write it. "Party" means "person." Cool, huh? We're each a PARTY!)

I, _____, promise to ONLY write to my best friend, _____, via email and postal mail. The following exceptions will hereby be made:

One (1) Skype session on the party's birthday.

Each party will be given one (1) phone call or Skype session per year in addition to a birthday.

The parties will decide a time to visit in the next two (2) years. This will be decided with the help of their parents.

Signed: _____

What do you think?

Love,

Molly

SEND

Chapter 11

Lost and Found

Olive

My ankle throbbed. A lot. Probably because my heart was going to beat out of my chest. I leaned on my crutches and looked up at my mom. She raised an eyebrow. I sighed and knocked on the door. This was going to be about as fun as spraining my ankle.

A woman opened the door. "Yes?" she said. "May I help you?"

Mom looked at me. Boy, she was not going to make this easy.

"I'm Olive. Is Mr. Anderson here?" I asked.

Mom added, "We have something he lost. My daughter and yours play on the same soccer team."

The woman smiled. "Oh, hi there! Come in. What happened to your foot, Olive?"

"I sprained my ankle," I said.

Mrs. Anderson made a face. "Ooh, I've done that before. Really hurts! You must be an awfully good person to hobble over here just to return something."

I closed my eyes and slowly shook my head. "I don't think so."

"Racie's playing out back," Mrs. Anderson said. "I'll go get her. Steven! Come in here! You've got company!"

Racie's dad came into the room. "Well, hello! What brings you here today?"

I swallowed hard and pulled the bracelet out of my pocket.

Racie's dad gasped and fell back onto the couch. It was like a big gust of wind had knocked him over. He covered his mouth for a second and then said, "Oh, my goodness. Where did you find this? Oh, you wonderful girl! Thank you!"

He rushed over and gave me a hug. He was so happy! I handed him the bracelet,

but I couldn't look him in the eye. He quickly put it in a desk drawer so his wife wouldn't see it.

"Well, that's it!" I said. "Time to go."

Mom put her hand on my shoulder and cleared her throat. Time for me to tell the truth. Ugh.

"Mr. Anderson," I said, "I've had it this whole time. I'm really sorry. I found it at practice and was going to sell it to go to New York City, but then you came over and said you lost it. And I felt bad.

SORRy

I should have told you then, but I couldn't, and then I sprained my ankle. I can't go to New York City anyway now, but I knew I needed to tell you. It was totally wrong to keep it."

I sniffed. Tears wouldn't stop running down my face. Although I was crying, I really did feel better for giving back the bracelet.

Racie's dad leaned forward. "Olive, you did the right thing now, and that's what counts. Thank you." He leaned forward more and dug in his back pocket. "In fact, I should really give you a reward."

I shook my head quickly. "No," I said. "Really. I'm just glad you have it back."

Mom squeezed me, and I knew I'd made the right choice.

Just then I heard two sets of footsteps coming down the hallway — Racie and her mom. Racie already knew I was TERRIBLE at soccer. Now she was about to find out I was a thief too.

But what I saw next almost knocked me out: Racie was wearing my sweater from Grandma.

RACIE!!!

MY SWEATER

Chapter 12

Molly Turns Ten

Molly

Dear Molly,

I signed the contract and dropped it in the mail!
You should see it soon. AND this means WE GET TO
SKYPE ON SATURDAY! I'm so excited!

Lots to tell you . . .

I gave the bracelet back to Racie's dad. He was SO
thankful! He even tried to give me money for a
reward, but I didn't take it.

And I sprained my ankle. I'm on crutches and everything. I cried. That's how bad it hurt. I have to be off my ankle for a week, and then it will take six weeks to heal. No soccer for a while, but Dad said we could watch practices together.

Funny story: When I found that bracelet at the field, my sweater fell out of my bag. But I didn't know it. My grandma had made it for me. I couldn't find it anywhere. I was so sad! When Mom and I went over to Racie's house, guess what? SHE WAS WEARING THE SWEATER! She saw it at the soccer field and thought it was pretty. So she kept it. We both laughed pretty hard about that. She got in trouble for not turning it in, just like me.

I can't wait for your party! Talk to you REALLY SOON!

Love,

Olive

I kept reading Olive's email over and over and over again. My birthday party was in two hours. Truthfully, I hardly even cared about it anymore. I was going to talk to Olive!

I felt nervous. I wondered if maybe Olive and I should talk by ourselves first. Just the two of us. I thought I'd ask Mom what she thought. So I went into the kitchen. Mom was hurrying to finish up the cupcakes.

"Mom," I said, "um . . . what do you think if I . . . or what if Olive and I sort of . . ."

"Molly, honey. I'm kind of busy here with the cupcakes. Spit it out."

I swallowed. "I think I want Olive to myself," I said.

Mom stopped frosting and smiled. Sometimes she really understands me. "You mean, you don't want to try to Skype *at* your birthday party."

I nodded.

"I think that's just fine," she said. "The first time you two talk should be private."

"Thanks, Mom," I called, running to my room. I quickly wrote to Olive.

Hi, Olive,

What do you think about talking by ourselves the first time — not at the party. Would you be mad?

Love,

Molly

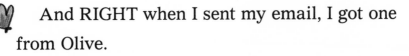

And RIGHT when I sent my email, I got one from Olive.

Dear Molly,

I think I want to talk to just you first. But it's your birthday. And we should do what you want. What do you think?

XOXOXO,

Olive

SEND MORE MAIL

I laughed out loud and emailed her again.
It was decided. We would talk at 8:00 my time.
Right before bed.

The party was SO much fun. I bounced
until my guts almost fell out. We played soccer,
and I beat the boys by a mile. Plus I got some
pretty great presents. But my best present was
waiting for me at 8:00.

At 7:50 I was fidgeting all over the place. I didn't know time could go so slow! I walked around and around my room. Mom came in and sat down on the bed.

"Birthday Girl, I know it's almost time for your big call," she said. "I'll be quick. I have one last present for you today."

She'd already gotten me two awesome videogames, a soccer net practice game, some clothes, and a book. *Another* present?

Best Birthday

Mom smiled super big and held out a piece of paper. It looked like a printed email. She'd written me a letter?

But then I read the page: "Two tickets to Sioux City, Iowa. Date???"

I looked up at my mom, my mouth wide open. "Are you joking?" I asked.

"Nope. We're going to Iowa to visit Olive!"

I screamed so loud that my mom plugged her ears. I leaped onto my bed and jumped up and down. I bounced so hard I nearly bounced Mom off!

"THANK YOU! THANK YOU! This is the best birthday ever!"

I hugged my mom super, super tight. Just then the Skype noise sounded on my computer. Olive was calling.

Mom gave me one last squeeze and walked to the door. She looked back with a smile and said, "NOW it will be."

About the Author

Megan Atwood lives and works in Minneapolis, Minnesota. She has written more than 35 children's books and teaches creative writing at Hamline University. When she is not writing books or teaching, she is inflicting love and affection on her cats and dreaming up more characters to keep her company. She also is trying to find more time to write personal letters to her loved ones, much like Molly and Olive.

Megan Atwood

About the Illustrator

Lucy Fleming lives and works in a small town in England with an animator and a black cat. She has been an avid doodler and bookworm since early childhood, drawing every day, bringing characters and stories to life. She never dreamed that illustrating would be her job! When not at her desk, Lucy loves to be outdoors in the sunshine with a cup of hot tea — doodling, of course.

Lucy Fleming

Glossary

accidentally—without meaning to

anniversary—a date people remember because an important event took place on that day

bauble—a showy piece of jewelry of little value

contract—a written or spoken agreement

exception—something to which the rules do not apply

expensive—costing a lot of money; not cheap

feed—food for animals

fidget—to wiggle or twitch repeatedly

four square—a ball game played by four people on a court divided into four squares

ID—something that proves who a person is; short for "identification"

ruin—to wreck beyond repair

seriously—not lightly

shin guard—a pad that protects the shin (the front of the lower leg) while playing some sports

sprain—an injury caused by the stretching or tearing of muscle or tissue

Talk It Out

1. What steps did Molly and Olive take to try to sell the bracelet?

2. Olive was offered a reward for turning in the bracelet, but she refused it. Do you think she should have accepted the money? Why or why not?

3. What do you think Olive meant when she said that seeing Mr. Anderson made him more "real"?

Write It Out

1. Rewrite the story to show what would've happened if Olive had turned in the bracelet when she found it.

2. Rewrite the story to show what would've happened if the girls had actually sold the bracelet for $600.

3. Describe your greatest treasure.

A Letter for You!

Dear friend,

Remember how I sprained my ankle? Well, you won't believe it, but I actually MISS soccer practice. Maybe Molly is rubbing off on me!

Molly plays on a "club" team — a team that travels places. I think I'll need to do a lot more practicing before I can do that! But I can see why Molly likes it. It feels good to be a part of a team. It's the same with me and gymnastics. Playing sports is super fun. Do you play any sports? What's your favorite? Are you a soccer fan like Molly?

Thanks, as always, for reading!

Your friend,

Olive

The fun doesn't stop here!

Discover more at www.capstonekids.com

Videos & Contests

Games & Puzzles

Friends & Favorites

Authors & Illustrators

Find cool websites and more books like this one at www.facthound.com. Just type in the Book ID: 9781479586936 and you're ready to go!